To my children and to all children
—T. T.

*For MonteQarlo, a queer angel who taught me to be myself, embrace my fluidity,
love my community, and never stop making art. Rest in power, my friend.*
—N. G.

Henry Holt and Company, *Publishers since 1866*
Henry Holt® is a registered trademark of Macmillan Publishing Group, LLC
175 Fifth Avenue, New York, NY 10010
mackids.com

Text copyright © 2019 by Theresa Thorn
Illustrations copyright © 2019 by Noah Grigni
All rights reserved.

Library of Congress Cataloging-in-Publication Data

Names: Thorn, Theresa, author. | Grigni, Noah, illustrator.
Title: It feels good to be yourself : a book about gender identity / Theresa Thorn ; illustrated by Noah Grigni.
Description: First edition. | New York : Henry Holt and Company, [2019]
Identifiers: LCCN 2018038732 | ISBN 978-1-250-30295-3 (hardcover)
Subjects: LCSH: Gender nonconformity—Juvenile literature. | Gender identity—Juvenile literature.
Classification: LCC HQ77.9 .T497 2019 | DDC 305.3—dc23
LC record available at https://lccn.loc.gov/2018038732

Our books may be purchased in bulk for promotional, educational, or business use.
Please contact your local bookseller or the Macmillan Corporate and Premium Sales Department at
(800) 221-7945 ext. 5442 or by email at MacmillanSpecialMarkets@macmillan.com.

First edition, 2019 / Designed by Liz Dresner
The artist used watercolor, gouache, and ink to create the illustrations in this book.
Printed in China by Hung Hing Off-set Printing Co. Ltd., Heshan City, Guangdong Province

1 3 5 7 9 10 8 6 4 2

IT FEELS GOOD TO BE YOURSELF

A BOOK ABOUT GENDER IDENTITY

WRITTEN BY THERESA THORN   ILLUSTRATED BY NOAH GRIGNI

Henry Holt and Company • New York

This is **RUTHiE**.

She's a transgender girl.

That means when she was born, everyone thought she was a boy. Until she grew a little older—old enough to tell everyone that she's actually a girl.

GiRL is Ruthie's gender identity.

This is Ruthie's brother, **XAVIER**.
Xavier is a cisgender boy.

That means when Xavier was born, everyone thought he was a boy, and as he grew older, it turned out everyone was right—he is a boy.

BOY is Xavier's gender identity.

There are so many different ways to be a boy or a girl—too many to fit in a book!

But not everyone feels like either a boy or a girl.

NON-BiNARY is a helpful word that can describe a kid who doesn't feel exactly like a boy or a girl.

This is Ruthie's friend **ALEX**.

Alex is **BOTH A BOY AND A GIRL**.

When Alex was born, everyone thought Alex was a girl, but Alex is both boy and girl. This is Alex's gender identity.

This is Alex's friend **JJ**.

JJ is NEITHER A BOY NOR A GIRL.

Ever since JJ was very little, they never felt exactly like a boy or a girl—they just felt like themself. This is JJ's gender identity.

Alex and JJ are both **NON-BINARY**.
Just like there are many different ways to
be a boy or a girl, there are many different
ways to be non-binary—too many to fit in a
book!

Some kids feel like girls. Some kids feel like boys.
Some kids feel like a little bit of both—part boy, part girl.

Some kids don't feel exactly like a boy or a girl—they feel like neither. Some kids feel that their gender identity isn't always the same—it's often changing.

And even with all these possible ways to be, some kids don't feel any of the words they know fit them exactly right. There are a never-ending number of ways to be yourself in the world.

Whether you feel like a boy, a girl, both, or neither, or if you describe yourself another way, that is your gender identity.

Your gender identity might match what people thought you were when you were born.

Or, it might not.

See, when you were born, you couldn't tell people who you were or how you felt. They looked at you and made a guess. Maybe they got it right, maybe they got it wrong.

What a baby's body looks like
when they're born can be a clue
to what the baby's gender will
be, but not always.

When people guess wrong, it's okay to let them know. Ruthie was five when she told her parents.

I know you think I'm a boy but really I feel like a girl.

Oops! Ruthie was a girl all along—
they just didn't know it at first.

When people guess right, it's also okay to let them know.

Xavier was three and and a half when he told his family.

I'm a boy! I like being a boy!

You might feel like a boy. You might feel like a girl. You might feel like both boy and girl—or like neither. You might feel like your gender changes from day to day or from year to year.

Your feelings about your gender are real. Listen to your heart.

No matter what your gender identity is, you are okay exactly the way you are. And you are loved.

It feels good to be **YOURSELF**, doesn't it?

SOME HELPFUL TERMS TO KNOW

SEX ASSIGNED AT BIRTH: This is what is listed on a newborn baby's birth certificate. Adults involved in the baby's birth say whether the baby appears female or male.

INTERSEX: Not all people's bodies are exactly male or female. Intersex means that, from birth, someone's body doesn't match exactly what we have defined as male or female.

GENDER IDENTITY: This is who you feel like within yourself—whether you feel like a boy, a girl, some combination of boy and girl, or something else. Your gender identity is who you know yourself to be. It might match your sex assigned at birth or it might not.

GENDER EXPRESSION: This is how you choose to present yourself to the world—which clothes you wear, how you style your hair, how you walk and talk. Gender expression is how you express your gender identity. There are a never-ending number of ways to express your gender identity—too many to fit in a book!

CISGENDER: This is when your gender identity matches your sex assigned at birth.

TRANSGENDER: This is when your gender identity is different from your sex assigned at birth.

NON-BINARY: This is a way to describe many identities that fall between boy and girl or outside the binary of boy and girl. There cannot be one definition, because there is no one way to be non-binary.

A NOTE ABOUT PRONOUNS

She/her, he/him, they/them, and ze/hir are some of the pronouns people of different gender identities may use to refer to themselves and would like others to use when talking to or about them. We can't know for sure what anyone's gender identity is just by looking at them or listening to them speak, and we can't know for sure which pronouns they use either. When we guess or assume and use the wrong words, we can really hurt people. A good first step is to listen. Someone who already knows a person well will probably use the correct pronouns when referring to that person, and we can follow their lead. It can be okay to ask about pronouns, but it is important to be sensitive. It might not be the right time or place to ask, or the person may not be ready to talk about it. If we introduce ourselves and share the pronouns we use, we can make it easier for the person we are meeting to do the same, if they feel comfortable.

SOME HELPFUL RESOURCES

BOOKS FOR KIDS

The Gender Identity Workbook for Kids: A Guide to Exploring Who You Are by Kelly Storck, LCSW; illustrated by Noah Grigni

I Am Jazz by Jessica Herthel and Jazz Jennings; illustrated by Shelagh McNicholas

Introducing Teddy: A Gentle Story About Gender and Friendship by Jessica Walton; illustrated by Dougal MacPherson

From the Stars in the Sky to the Fish in the Sea by Kai Cheng Thom; illustrated by Wai-Yant Li and Kai Yun Ching

Julián Is a Mermaid by Jessica Love

Who Are You?: The Kid's Guide to Gender Identity by Brook Pessin-Whedbee; illustrated by Naomi Bardoff

MORE HELPFUL RESOURCES

BOOKS FOR ADULTS

Gender Born, Gender Made: Raising Healthy Gender-Nonconforming Children by
   Diane Ehrensaft, PhD

Raising the Transgender Child: A Complete Guide for Parents, Families, and Caregivers
   by Michele Angello and Ali Bowman

DOCUMENTARY FILM

Gender Revolution: A Journey with Katie Couric

ORGANIZATIONS AND HELPLINES

Gender Spectrum
   genderspectrum.org

PFLAG
   pflag.org

Human Rights Campaign
   hrc.org

GLAAD
   glaad.org

Trans Youth Equality Foundation
   transyouthequality.org

The Trevor Project
   TrevorLifeline: 866-488-7386
   thetrevorproject.org

Trans Lifeline
   US: 877-565-8860 / Canada: 877-330-6366
   translifeline.org

AUTHOR'S NOTE

My daughter was five when she told me she wasn't the gender I'd assumed she was at birth. Actually, she told me even earlier, but she was five when I started listening.

Learning about gender diversity and my daughter has been a lesson in the value of withholding judgment. My daughter's gender identity and expression are personal and unique to her; they have very little to do with me or my opinions, assumptions, and preconceptions. I wanted to give my daughter a book in which she could see herself. A book that reflected her back without judgment. I wanted, further, to give that experience to all kids. I wanted a book that is less about accepting one child's difference and more about celebrating the amazing diversity of all children.

It is my wish that this book helps children to better understand themselves and others, and that it facilitates conversations within families. This book is for trans kids, cis kids, non-binary kids, gender-fluid kids, gender-expansive kids, questioning kids, and all kids, everywhere.

—Theresa Thorn

ILLUSTRATOR'S NOTE

I was fourteen when I came out as trans, and I'm lucky to have parents who listened and stood up for me when others failed to. My transition is not linear or binary. For me, transitioning is a fluid, lifelong process of personal discovery and self-actualization. It means staying true to all parts of myself and evolving on my own terms, as someone who is masculine, feminine, both, and neither.

I illustrated this book because it's a resource I wish I had as a kid. Language is power. Growing up in Georgia without access to words like transgender and non-binary, I struggled to define myself from a young age, and I felt isolated and unseen. I painted as a way of processing my dysphoria. Now, I'm painting to connect with my community, celebrate queer resilience, and embrace a radically inclusive future.

We need more books with trans protagonists. The trans population is as diverse as the human population, and no number of books could hold all our stories. Dear reader, it's up to you to continue this work, rewrite these definitions, share your stories, and build a future more expansive than we can imagine. You are the future we're fighting for.

—Noah Grigni

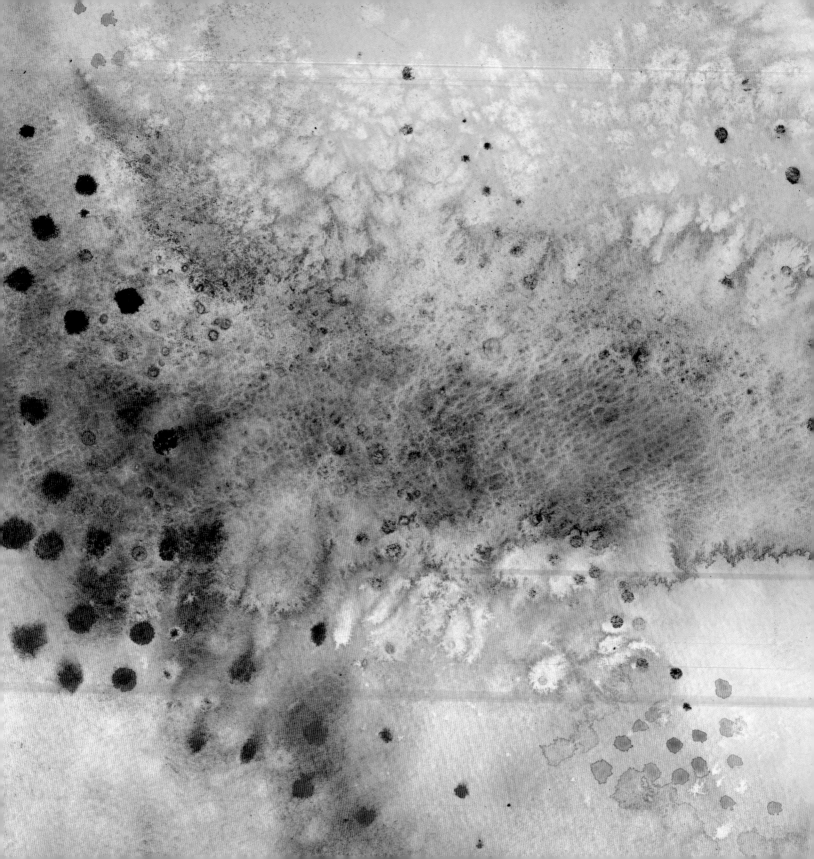